More Than One

By
Miriam Schlein
Pictures by
Donald Crews

Greenwillow Books, New York

Library of Congress Cataloging-in-Publication Data

Schlein, Miriam.
More than one / by Miriam Schlein ; pictures by Donald Crews.
    p.   cm.
Summary: Explains how the number one can refer to a single item, the two shoes in a pair, the seven days in a week, the twelve eggs in a dozen, all the trees in a forest, and much more.
ISBN 0-688-14102-1 (trade).
ISBN 0-688-14103-X (lib. bdg.)
1. Counting—Juvenile literature.
[1. One (The number).
2. Number concept.
3. Counting.]
I. Crews, Donald, ill.
II. Title.   QA113.S385
1996   513—dc20
95-38136   CIP   AC

ONE sun
in the sky.

ONE whale in the water. Can **ONE** be more than **1**?

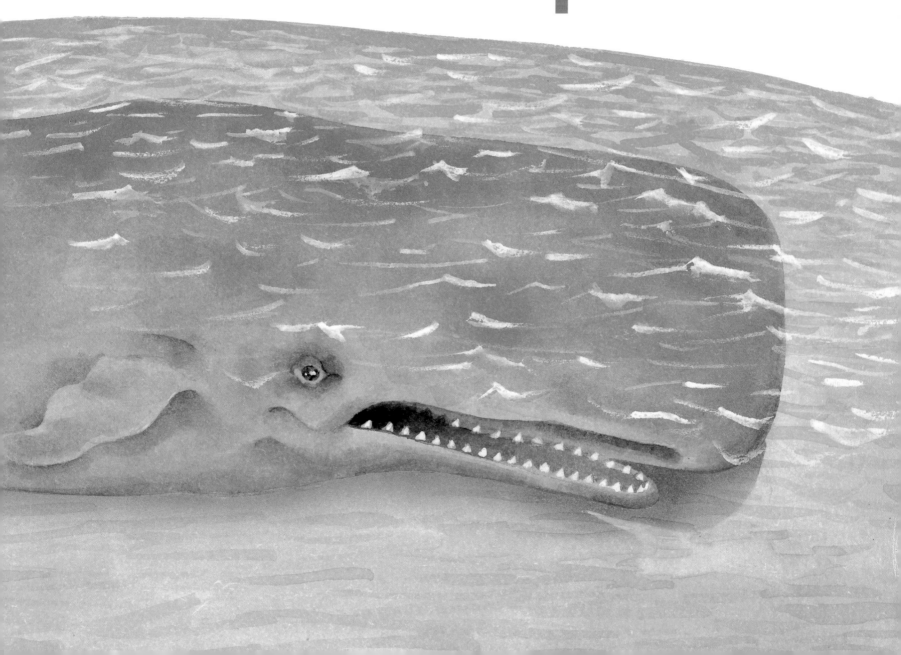

YES!

Here is ONE PAIR of shoes.

How many shoes in ONE PAIR of shoes?

ONE PAIR of shoes is TWO SHOES.

2

Whether they're
on your feet or
under the bed–
a pair is always
two. **2**

Can **ONE** be
more than that?

YES! **ONE WEEK is SEVEN DAYS.**
Can ONE be more than that?

7

One right after the other.

YES! ONE BASEBALL TEAM is NINE PLAYERS.

9

Count them.

Can ONE be more than that?

YES!
ONE DOZEN
eggs is
TWELVE.

12

Twelve eggs.
Twelve eggs
all together.

Can ONE
be different,
different
every time?

YES! ONE FAMILY
can be TWO PEOPLE,
2

THREE PEOPLE,
3

FOUR PEOPLE,
4

or FIVE,
5

or SIX,

6

**or more.
How many
in your
family?**

ONE FLOCK of birds can have lots of birds. It's awfully hard to count them.

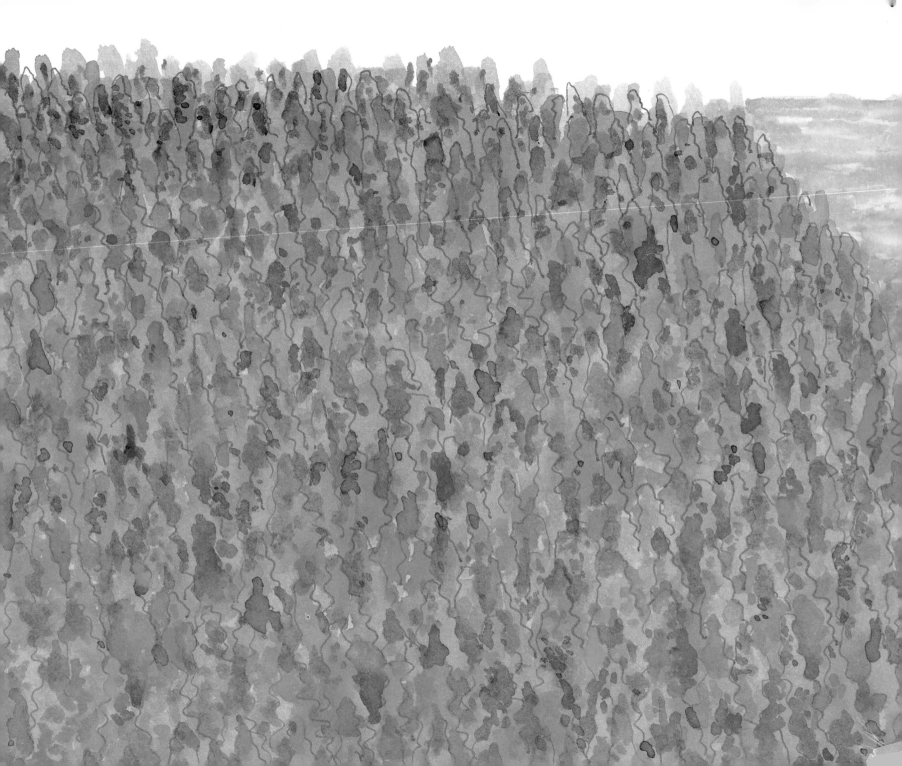

ONE FOREST
has lots of
trees.

ONE OCEAN
has billions
and trillions
and skadillions
of drops of water.

But they are still just
ONE FLOCK,
ONE FOREST,
ONE OCEAN.

ONE CROWD
of kids is made
up of lots more
than one.

And
ONE BEACH
can have
so many
bits of sand,
you couldn't
count them
even if you sat
there counting
for a day,
a week,
a month,
or even a year....

ONE,
TWO,
THREE,
FOUR.
ONE can be **1**
and
ONE can be
more.